FLICKA, RICKA, DICKA

Go to Market

FLICKA, RICKA, DICKA
Go to Market

BY MAJ LINDMAN

ALBERT WHITMAN & COMPANY
CHICAGO, ILLINOIS

Flicka, Ricka, and Dicka and their family had moved away from the city.

The little girls were very happy. They liked to play out of doors.

One day Ricka said, "We live a long way from town!"

"How will we get to school?" asked Flicka.

"If only we had bicycles," said Dicka. "But I am sure that Father can't afford them."

"Here is a seed catalog. It may help you."

"It would be fun to earn some money," said Ricka.

"Then we could buy our own bicycles!" cried Flicka and Dicka together. "But how can we do it?"

Father had been listening. Now he handed the girls a pretty book. "Here is a seed catalog. It may help you."

"Oh, Father, do you think we can grow a garden?"

"Yes," said Father, "but you will have to work hard."

The girls made a list of all the good things they would grow.

"Carrots!" said Flicka.

"Radishes!" said Ricka.

"Lettuce!" said Dicka.

"My, but I am hungry already," laughed Father. "What about peas and beans and parsley, too?"

"We must grow things that we can sell," said Flicka.

So they wrote a letter and sent for their seeds. They waited.

While they waited they worked hard, weeding, hoeing, raking. Soon they had a large square of black earth ready. Where were the seeds?

They worked hard.

At last the seeds arrived.

"Oh," said Ricka, "even the outsides of the envelopes are beautiful."

Now they had to decide where to plant the different vegetables.

Father helped the girls. To make straight rows he tied a long string to two pegs. Flicka held one peg. Ricka held the other.

Dicka took a stick and drew it along the ground following the string.

"This is the path for the seeds," said Dicka.

"It is a good furrow," said Father. "Many of them will be needed. You must mark each row. Put the seed envelope on a stick at the end of the row."

The girls put the seeds into the long rows. They covered the seeds with the black earth.

"This is the path for the seeds," said Dicka.

They tied them to poles.

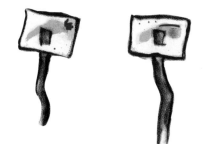

"Will they be up by Sunday?" Ricka asked. Everyone laughed.

"You can do something else while you wait," said Father. "You can plant some things that are started."

Father helped them buy some tomato plants, some cucumber and some melon plants. Flicka asked, "What is this long, beautiful plant with the big leaves?"

"Fine big orange pumpkins will grow on that vine," said Father.

Flicka, Ricka, and Dicka put their new plants into the ground.

They tied the tomato plants to poles. The new plants seemed to feel at home and they grew well.

Then came the day when the peas and beans and parsley put their heads through the ground.

Now Flicka, Ricka, and Dicka were busy every minute. They watered their garden in the morning and at night. They watched for weeds and pulled out every one.

"It is hard work," said Flicka.

"The garden is growing, but it is growing slowly," said Ricka.

"I wonder if we will really get our bicycles," said Dicka.

They stopped work and looked at each other. It was a very hot day and it seemed like a long time before they would have vegetables to sell at market. Suddenly, "Good morning," said a quiet voice.

"Good morning," said a quiet voice.

The day came when they could gather the first vegetables.

"You can call me Uncle Bertie," said a man on the other side of the garden fence. "I live on the little farm next to yours."

Flicka, Ricka, and Dicka were glad to have a new friend. They liked Uncle Bertie's nice smile.

"I have a pony and cart that could be used," he said. "How would you like to sell my flowers for me? Then you may take your vegetables and my flowers to market in the cart!"

The girls were very happy with this plan. Now they had a way to get to market.

Then the day came when they could gather the first vegetables. The next day they would be going to market.

The girls took turns driving Folly.

It was Saturday. The girls were up early. There was still the lettuce to cut so that it would be as fresh as possible for market.

Uncle Bertie arrived with the pony and cart.

"This is Folly," said Uncle Bertie. "She is as gentle as a lamb."

The little brown mare lowered her head and seemed to say, "hello."

"I hope you can sell these flowers at market," said Uncle Bertie.

"Oh, we will try," said Flicka, Ricka, and Dicka.

How beautiful the cart looked loaded with Uncle Bertie's flowers and the crisp, fresh vegetables.

The girls took turns driving Folly. The little brown mare trotted along happily.

It was noisy and busy in the marketplace. At first the girls felt a little shy.

"I think that I will hide behind the vegetables," said Ricka. Flicka and Dicka knew that she was joking but felt timid, too.

Then some friendly, smiling people began to ask them about the parsley, the beans, and the peas. Soon they were too busy to think about themselves.

The cash box they had taken with them was getting heavier and heavier.

"There," said Flicka. "I have sold the last bunch of Uncle Bertie's beautiful flowers."

"We must pick more parsley next time," said Ricka. "We were sold out an hour ago."

Soon everything had been sold!

Soon they were too busy to think about themselves.

"It is lucky we brought a big umbrella."

A surprise was waiting for Flicka, Ricka, and Dicka now.

Folly and the cart had been left in a parking yard just outside the marketplace.

But there was not a sign of Folly and the cart.

"I guess I did not fasten the rope very well," said Dicka.

"She will find her way home," said Flicka. "But we must leave our boxes and crates."

"We will have to carry the heavy cash box," said Ricka.

"Yes, we can take turns," said Dicka. "And it is lucky we brought a big umbrella. Hear that thunder!"

"Good!" cried the three tired little girls. "Tonight we will not have to water our garden!"

Yes, Folly found her way home. Uncle Bertie showed the girls how to fasten her to a fence. After that she was always waiting with the cart when market day was over.

Every Saturday, Flicka, Ricka, and Dicka went to market, and at last they had their fall crop ready to take with them.

"These pumpkins are bigger than your heads," laughed Father.

"Such fine tomatoes and melons," said their mother. "We are really proud of our girls!"

The people who came to market had become their friends. The three little girls were not shy now.

They always sold all of Uncle Bertie's flowers and all of their vegetables every Saturday.

The three little girls were not shy now.

Now the harvest was over. The girls had
gone to market for the last time.

"We must do something for Uncle Bertie
and his wife. And we must give Folly a present,
too," they said to Father.

"A box of lump sugar for Folly," said Father.
"That will please her."

"For Uncle Bertie?" he said. "Well, what
about a big basket of your very own
vegetables? I believe that would really please
Uncle Bertie and his wife."

They took their presents to their friends
and hurried home. They were eager to count
their money.

"Sugar in lumps for Folly!"

Flicka, Ricka, and Dicka were all riding bicycles!

"I hope we have enough money for our bicycles," said Ricka.

Father took down their money box.

Yes, there was really enough money!

Soon Flicka, Ricka, and Dicka were all riding bicycles!

They had grown a garden, and they had
earned their very own bicycles.

They had grown a garden.

The FLICKA, RICKA, DICKA BOOKS
By MAJ LINDMAN

Library of Congress Cataloging-in-Publication Data

Lindman, Maj.
Flicka, Ricka, Dicka go to market / written and illustrated by Maj Lindman.
p. cm.
Summary: Three little Swedish girls cultivate a big vegetable garden, sell their crops each Saturday
at the market, and earn money for bicycles.
[1. Gardening—Fiction. 2. Sisters—Fiction. 3. Triplets—Fiction. 4. Markets—Fiction.
5. Moneymaking projects—Fiction. 6. Sweden—Fiction.] I. Title.
PZ7.L659Fo 2012
[E]—dc22
2011008565

Text and illustrations copyright © 1958, 1979 by Albert Whitman & Company
Based on original design by Stephanie Bart-Horvath
Published in the United States of America in 2011 by Albert Whitman & Company
ISBN 978-0-8075-2478-7 (hardcover)
ISBN 978-0-8075-2477-0 (ebook)

Printed in China
10 9 8 7 6 5 4 3 WKT 24 23 22 21 20

For more information about Albert Whitman & Company,
visit our website at www.albertwhitman.com